P9-CFG-641

SEP 2 8 2010

WITHDRAWN
Baldwinsville, NY 13027-2575

Kindergarten Diary

as told to

Antoinette Portis

by me, Annalina

HARPER
An Imprint of HarperCollins*Publishers*

Good job!

Kindergarten Diary

Copyright © 2010 by Antoinette Portis

Manufactured in China.

All rights reserved. No part of this book may be used or reproduced in any manner whatsoever without

written permission except in the case of brief quotations embodied in critical articles and reviews.

For informationaddress HarperCollins Children's Books, a division of HarperCollins Publishers,

10 East 53rd Street, New York, NY 10022.

www.harpercollinschildrens.com

SEP 2 8 2010

Library of Congress Cataloging-in-Publication Data

Portis, Antoinette.

Kindergarten diary / as told to Antoinette Portis by me, Annalina.—1st ed.

p.   cm.

Summary: Annalina's diary entries reflect her feelings and experiences as she goes from being afraid

to go to kindergarten to loving it during her first month of school.

ISBN 978-0-06-145691-6 (trade bdg.) — ISBN 978-0-06-145692-3 (lib. bdg.)

[1. Kindergarten—Fiction.   2. Schools—Fiction.   3. Diaries—Fiction.]   I. Title

PZ7.P8362 Ki   2010   2009006184

[E]—dc22   CIP

                                                                                                            AC

Typography by Martha Rago

10   11   12   13   14   LEO   10 9 8 7 6 5 4 3 2 1   ❖ First Edition

For Alexandra "The Fooster" Portis,
monkey-bar and hand-ball master

Thanks to Ms. Deborah Craig
and her kindergarten class

Thank you, Michael

I don't want to go to kindergarten!
I only like preschool.
I don't want to go to Big School with big kids.

What if they're mean?

me

BIG BOY

My mom says I *have* to
go to Big School.

So here is what I am
going to wear:
my rainbow bathing suit,
my ballet skirt,
my plaid shirt,
my cowboy boots,
and definitely no socks.

My mom says I have to
look *nice* today.

And I have to wear socks.

September 2½
Still the First Day

My mom walked me to my classroom and held my hand hard. The teacher made all the grown-ups leave.

Hardly anybody cried.

Then we sat on the rug.
We are room 2K.
We are fine!

I was worried my teacher would be scary.

But she is very un-scary.
Her name is Dorothy Duffy
and her nickname is Dot.

We call her

Ms. Duffy

(Her brother used to
call her Polka Dot.)

Welcome,
Rm. 2K

September 4

We have our own playground. The big kids aren't allowed to come in!

Today we pretended the monkey bars were in the jungle. One boy went all the way across.

Then I tried and I fell
off and the alligators
almost ate me.

(The pretend
alligators.)

September 5

Today I made a farm with blocks and cows. Ms. Duffy said I had to share.

I wanted the cows to be all mine!

Then
David M. and me
made a
very,
very,
very big
tower of cows.

He's coming
over to my
house
to play
tomorrow.

He can
whistle!

We are practicing
writing our names.

Annalina takes
too many letters!

I am going to
change my name to

and save the
lina
for when I am bigger.

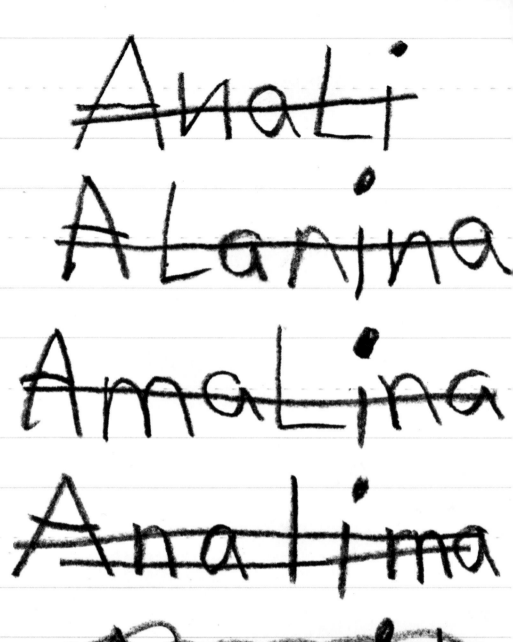

Me and Zoe played at recess today. Zoe likes socks. She always wears something pink. She let me use her extra jump rope.

It's pink.

September 10

Today we pretended the monkey bars were on a spaceship and you had to hold on or you would float away forever.

David M. went all the way across forward and backward! I kept practicing, even though I got a blister.

I went almost all the
way across before I fell off.

Zoe saved me!

I was scared to go up and do show-and-tell in front of everyone. But then it was my turn.

I showed my doll shoes, red cowboy boots, yellow sneakers, green ice skates that my dog almost ate, a blue car—

Then Ms. Duffy said, "Thank you, Anna. Now let someone else have a turn."

I LOVE show-and-tell!

David M. is my best friend,
and also Zoe.

Zoe is afraid to touch a snail.

Maybe if snails were pink and
sparkly, she would like them.

September 15
Picture Day

My dad's scissors were sitting by the sink this morning and I got an idea.

It's harder to cut hair than I thought.

September 16

I brought an extra cookie in my lunch for Zoe.

I had to taste it to see if it was OK.

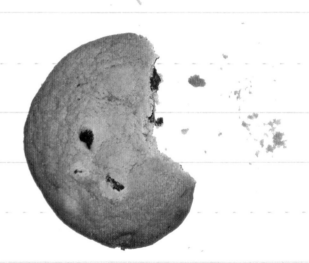

It was.

We have homework now like big kids.
This week it's finding pictures of
things that start with A.
Like Anna.

Poor Zoe.
She has to wait a
very
very
very long
time to get
to her letter.

Z

September 18

David M. said he was the best big-red-ball hitter in the whole world. We played at recess.

I beat him three times in a row.

September 19

David M. won't play big-red-ball with me anymore.

September 22

Happy birthday,
David M.!
We had a party at school
with cupcakes.

With LOTS of frosting.

September 23

We have a pet tortoise
in room 2K.

We feed her bugs
and tomatoes.

Guess who
got to name her?

Lucy Izzie Chunky-ola

BY Anna

September 24

I am definitely good
at the monkey bars—
I can go across forward
and backward without
stopping.

I am the second-best
monkey in the universe!

September 25

The first graders came over and
teased us for being little.

They think they're all grown up.
(Like they're 12.)

I asked Ms. Duffy, and she said
we have been in kindergarten
for almost a whole month.
That is a
very
very
very long time!

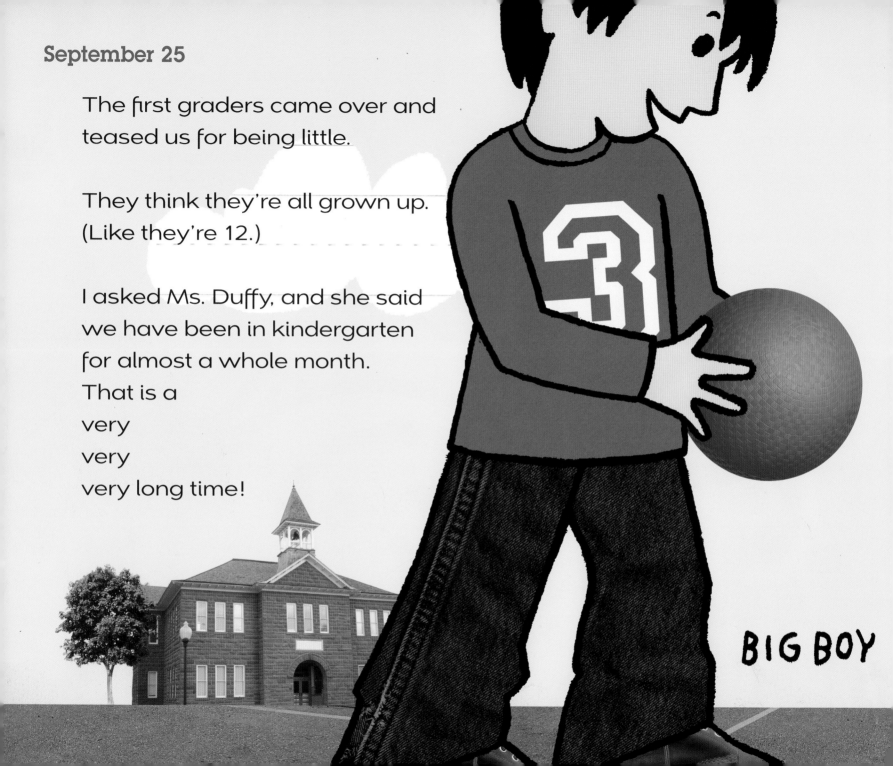

BIG BOY

When I am in first grade,
I am not going to be scared!

When I am in first grade,
I am not going to be mean!

un-mean me

kindergartner

un-scared me

kindergartner

September 29

But right now, I like Zoe and David M. and Ms. Duffy and the monkey bars and making tortoise pictures, and I definitely like kindergarten.

September 30
Too Busy to Write Any More!

P.S. We are room 2K. We are fine!